I waited, listening,  my secret weapon – my trusty penlight torch – out of one of my pyjama pockets.

Then, from under the bed, I heard it. A shuffling noise, ever so quiet but definitely there. It was a big one. I listened carefully until I could tell which way it was facing. And I was just about to leap out of bed and blast the monster away with a pencil-thin beam of battery-powered light, when it spoke.

"Jack?" it said. "It's me!"

Shortlisted for the Ottaker's Children's Book Prize

Also available by John Dougherty,
and published by Young Corgi Books:

ZEUS ON THE LOOSE
'Energetic and page-turning' *INK magazine*
Shortlisted for the Branford Boase Award

NITERACY HOUR
'A brilliant story that even boys will enjoy,
with delightful illustrations' *Daily Echo*

For more information about John Dougherty:
www.visitingauthor.com

Jack Slater Monster Investigator

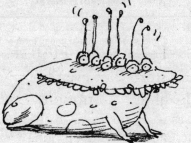

JOHN DOUGHERTY

Illustrated by Georgien Overwater

JACK SLATER – MONSTER INVESTIGATOR
A YOUNG CORGI BOOK 978 0 552 55372 8 (from January 2007)
0552 55372 7

Published in Great Britain by Young Corgi
an imprint of Random House Children's Books

This edition published 2006

1 3 5 7 9 10 8 6 4 2

Set in Bembo MT Schlbk

Young Corgi Books are published by Random House Children's Books,
61–63 Uxbridge Road, London W5 5SA,
a division of The Random House Group Ltd,
in Australia by Random House Australia (Pty) Ltd,
20 Alfred Street, Milsons Point, Sydney, NSW 2061, Australia,
in New Zealand by Random House New Zealand Ltd,
18 Poland Road, Glenfield, Auckland 10, New Zealand,
and in South Africa by Random House (Pty) Ltd,
Endulini, 5A Jubilee Road, Parktown 2193, South Africa

THE RANDOM HOUSE GROUP Limited Reg. No. 954009
www.**kids**at**randomhouse**.co.uk

A CIP catalogue record for this book is available from the British Library.

Printed and bound in Great Britain by
Bookmarque Ltd, Croydon, Surrey

To my own little monsters, with much love

Chapter One

I was just in the middle of a lovely dream when my bedroom door opened and the light from the landing woke me up.

I groaned and opened my eyes. Two timid-looking pyjama-clad figures stood there, shuffling sheepishly.

"Um . . . please can we sleep in your room tonight?" one of them said.

I groaned again, and sat up. "What's wrong?" I asked, even though I knew what the answer would be.

"There's a monster under our bed!"

Sighing, I swung my feet out of bed and into my slippers. This was the third time in a week, and I was starting to get a bit tired of it.

"All right," I said. "You two snuggle up in here and go back to sleep. I'll deal with the monster."

"Be careful, son," said the taller one.

"I will, Dad," I said. "Sleep well. 'Night, Mum."

I closed the bedroom door behind me, and switched the landing light off. My parents don't believe it, but a light *outside* the bedroom does nothing to keep monsters away. It just makes them harder to see.

Poor Mum and Dad, though. It can't be easy for them having a son who's – though I say it myself – the world's greatest Monster Investigator.

I took a deep breath when I reached their room. The big double bed was right against the furthest wall, and I had to get to it in under five seconds. Walking. One of the first things you learn as a Monster Investigator is that most of the stuff kids make up to keep monsters away *actually works*. Hands up if you've ever counted to five while you got into bed?

I thought so.

OK, I said to myself, here we go.

"One . . ." I counted aloud, stepping into the room.

"Two . . ." Walking as quickly as I could, but *not running*. You mustn't run, or they'll get you.

TWO . . .

"Three . . ." Nearly at the bed now, but I had to get *into* it by five. Properly under the covers, up to the shoulders.

"Four . . ." I reached the bed and jumped onto it.

Once you get to the bed, you can go as quickly as you like, but you have to keep counting, fair and square.

4

"Five!" Just in time, I snuggled down under the thick, warm duvet and breathed a sigh of relief. Not that I was *really* scared, of course – I'd like to see the monster that could get the better of me. But I wanted it to think I was.

I waited, listening, while my hand slipped my secret weapon – my trusty penlight torch – out of one of my pyjama pockets.

Then, from under the bed, I heard it. A shuffling noise, ever so quiet but definitely there. It was a big one. I listened carefully until I could tell which way it was facing. And I was just about to leap out of bed and blast the monster away with a pencil-thin beam of battery-powered light, when it spoke.

"Jack?" it said. "It's me!"

Recognizing the voice, I lowered my torch.

"Bernard!" I sighed, relieved. "What are *you* doing here?"

it's me!

Bernard was my best informant in the monster underworld. If anything big was going down, he'd hear about it – and then I'd hear about it. No question, he was really valuable to me.

He was also in one of his moods.

"Hey," he growled, "I've *told* you. Don't call me Bernard! I'm just a monster with no name! I mean, I reckon I deserve a bit of respect after all the help I've given you, and anyhow—"

Usually when Bernard – which *is* his name, by the way – gets going like this

I just listen, and wait till he's got it out of his system. But something told me we didn't have time for this.

"Not *now*, Bernard!" I interrupted.

"OK, OK," he muttered. "So do you want to hear the news, or don't you?"

I wanted to hear it, all right. Bernard had *never* appeared under my parents' bed before. Usually if he had some information for me, he'd leave a note under my bed asking me to switch off my monster-traps at, say, eight o'clock, and then he'd come through and talk to me. So for him just to appear in my house must have meant something that couldn't wait.

"Sure I do," I told him. "What's up?"

There was another shuffling noise. Then a sound like a drain being unblocked – which was, I realized after a moment, Bernard clearing his throat. Then, more shuffling.

It sounded like Bernard was nervous about something. Really nervous.

"Come on, Bernard, spit it out," I said.

This time, he didn't even notice me use his name. This was one rattled monster.

"OK, OK," he spat. "Listen up, kid, and listen good. Something big is going down – I mean *real* big. The word under the streets is: no more hiding under beds in the dark scaring itty-bitty little kids. The underworld is getting organized."

A cold feeling crept over my skin, like a wave of small determined spiders.

"What do you mean, organized?" I demanded. "Monsters don't organize! What have you always told me, Bernard? *It's a monster-eat-monster world down there! Every monster for himself!*"

"Not any more," he assured me. "Not all of us monsters is happy about it – but they got ways of making us . . . co-operate." As he said this, his voice trembled a little.

8

I suddenly realized – Bernard wasn't just nervous; he was terrified.

"Who's making you co-operate?" I said. "And co-operate with what?"

He gulped – a long slow noise like a snake swallowing a dromedary – and said:

"OK, Jack, listen real carefully. I'm gonna tell you the whole story. But the main thing you gotta know is—"

And then there was a sound like a thousand people screaming a long way off, and another sound like a huge heavy wooden door closing – *THUNK!*

Then there was silence.

"Bernard?" I said. "Bernard, are you OK?"

But Bernard didn't answer.

Chapter Two

Clutching my penlight torch, I leaped off the bed and crouched down low.

"Bernard?" I said again.

Still no answer.

I kept one thumb firmly on the switch of the torch and my eyes glued to the dark space under Mum and Dad's bed. With the other hand I grabbed a toy sword and waved it around where Bernard should have been.

Nothing. The space under the bed was empty. Bernard was gone.

Assuming, of course, that he was as big as I'd always thought. I'd never actually seen him.

Just in case, I said, "Bernard? If you *are* still there, time to go, because I'm going to count to five and then switch the torch on. OK? One . . . two . . . three . . . four . . . FIVE!"

I flicked the switch.

There was nothing there.

Nothing except a lot of fluff and a crumpled piece of paper.

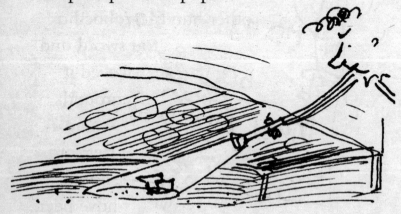

I swept the torch-beam left and right, just to be certain, and then reached in and took the piece of paper. I left the fluff.

The piece of paper turned out to be a note. Written by a hand that obviously wasn't used to holding a pen – and probably wasn't the right shape for it anyway – it said:

BurNuds gonna
get his.
HaNd in yor
baj or
yool get yors.

Unfortunately, the next day was a school day. I woke up late, got to school late, and almost fell asleep in assembly. And I don't know how many times I got told off that morning for not listening in class.

The reason I don't know how many times I got told off for not listening, is that I wasn't listening. I was thinking.

I was thinking about Bernard, and wondering what he had been about to tell me.

I was thinking about the note – 'Hand in your badge' it had said. It meant, of course, my official Monster Investigator badge.

And I was thinking about the talk in the playground. One of the kids at school had just become the latest victim of the criminals they were calling Ghost Burglars – burglars who could get into a house without breaking any locks or windows.

Burglars who could sneak into your room without waking you, and steal all your newest, coolest stuff from right by your bed while you lay asleep.

I almost began to wonder if the Ghost Burglars could really be Monster Burglars – but none of the stuff they were stealing was of any use to a monster. Monsters don't wear designer clothes or expensive trainers; they can't watch DVDs or play computer games or even use a mobile phone because of the light from the screens.

No, the Ghost Burglars were someone else's problem. I had a problem of my own to solve.

A Missing Monster problem.

After school, I went to the Ministry.

The Ministry of Monsters is different from all the other government departments in a number of ways:

Firstly – it's a secret. Everyone knows there's a Minister in charge of schools; most grown-ups can tell you the name of the Minister in charge of prisons and police and so on; but hardly anyone would ever believe there's a Minister for Monsters.

Secondly – most of the other ministries have classy offices in Whitehall, up in the centre of London. The Ministry of Monsters is based in an expensive treehouse in the back garden of one of the posh houses a few streets away from where I live.

And thirdly – Clyde Pumfrey-Soames, Minister for Monsters, is the only government minister who hasn't grown up yet.

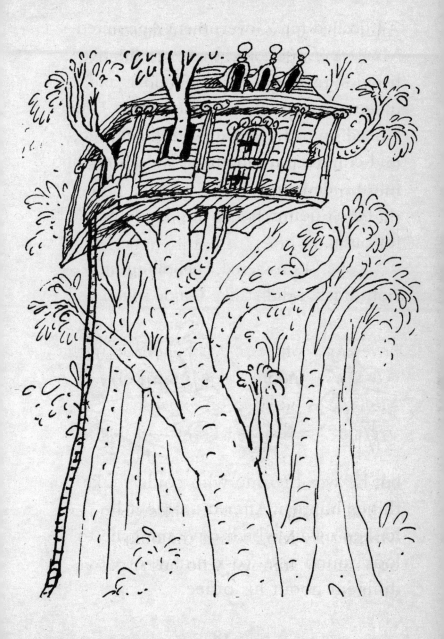

I flashed my 'Government Appointed Monster Investigator' badge at the two heavies guarding the rope ladder, and made my way up to Clyde's office. Clyde looked up as I entered, went bright red, and crammed a magazine he was reading into his desk drawer.

"Don't you ever knock?" he demanded furiously.

"Nope," I answered, eyeballing him right back. I didn't like Clyde much,

but he was the one who could make things happen. After a moment he looked away, which gave me time to look round and work out what was different about his office.

Not that it took much working out. Clyde's the most spoiled kid I know — probably the most spoiled kid *anybody* knows — but most of the expensive presents he gets given are, to be honest, pretty nerdy. I think his dad has firm ideas about what's "good" for a growing boy, and what isn't. Either that, or he's just got no taste at all.

Something, though, had obviously changed in the Pumfrey-Soames household. The office was piled high with incredibly cool stuff — too cool for Clyde, in my opinion, and *way* too cool for a treehouse. There was a widescreen plasma TV on the wall, for instance, and a brand new DVD player underneath it. He had all the latest movies in a rack nearby, too. Come to that, he looked a bit different himself — he was wearing much, much cooler and trendier clothes than usual, and a pair of the most expensive-looking trainers I'd ever seen.

19

before now

"Did Christmas come early, Clyde?" I asked him. "Or – no, don't tell me – *you're* the Ghost Burglar everyone's talking about!"

"Don't be stupid, Slater," Clyde scowled. "My dad's got enough money to buy me anything I want. You know that. Why would I need to steal?"

"Yeah, and how would you get into anyone's house without tripping over your own feet, anyway?" I retorted.

It's true about the money. Clyde's dad, you see, is a multi-millionaire – the boss of Pumfrey-Soames Furniture PLC.

You've seen the ads – 'Pumfrey-Soames for comfy homes'.

That's how come we have a Ministry of Monsters, in fact. Clyde's dad pays for everything – which is why Clyde gets to be the Minister. And being so rich and important, Mr Pumfrey-Soames even got his friend the Prime Minister to make the Ministry an official Government Department – on paper, at least. I'd never known Clyde to get quite so much stuff from his dad all at once, though. Maybe the old man was just in a good mood.

Unlike his little boy.

"So did you just come up here to give me cheek, Slater," he snapped, "or is there something I can do for you?"

It was time to get down to business. I explained about Bernard turning up in the middle of the night, and disappearing before he could finish warning me.

Clyde listened, nodding.

"Now the way I see it," I went on, "there are two things you could do. You could call all the registered Monster Investigators in the country and ask them what their informers are saying."

I paused. What I was about to suggest was going to sound crazy.

"Or you could send someone into the monster underworld to find out for themselves."

Chapter Three

Sending an Investigator into the monster underworld was the most dangerous idea I'd ever had, and I wasn't sure how Clyde would react.

I thought he might say, "No way. Too risky."

I thought he might say, "OK, Slater, see you when you get back – *if* you get back."

I thought he might say, "We need more information before I can agree to that."

He didn't say any of these things.

Instead, he leaned back, in this superior way he has – like he's trying to pretend he's not just a kid like the rest of us – and put his hands together like he was about to play "here's the church and here's the steeple". Then he smiled smugly, and said, "Don't you think you're taking all this a bit too seriously?"

Too seriously? If I was right, this would be the biggest thing the Ministry of Monsters had ever dealt with! I was just about to say, "Were you actually *listening*, Clyde?" when it hit me.

Clyde was trying to grow up.

And if he was trying to be more grown-up, then slowly but surely he was going to stop believing in monsters.

Because grown-ups *don't* believe in monsters under the bed. Even my mum and dad only believe in them when they're woken by one during the night; then in the morning they're all, *oh, silly us, what imaginations*. It's as if daylight does something to their brains. So if Clyde was trying to grow up, he was going to believe in monsters less and less.

Sure enough, he gave me
this big speech about how
maybe we should stop
playing games and
start trying to
properly help
all those
children
who were
scared of
monsters
"when
there's really
no reason
to be".

oh,
silly
me...

Then – all pleased with himself – he
showed me a glossy brochure. Something
he'd been working on.
"The sort of thing the Ministry should
really be doing," he said.

25

I have to admit it made sense, in a screwy kind of way.

It turns out that Clyde had designed this new bed for kids, and his dad liked it so much that Pumfrey-Soames Furniture had already made thousands of them.

"They'll be in the shops tomorrow!" Clyde said excitedly. "Dad loves the design! He says it'll be his biggest-selling bed ever – which, by the way, is the reason he's so pleased with me at the moment.

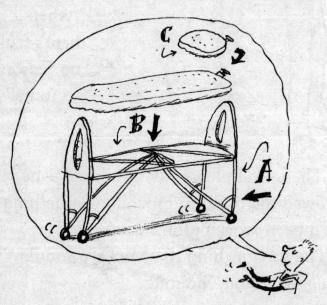

"The idea is, the bed is strong but really light, and it's on wheels. We call it the *skatebed*.

"The parents will all want them because it's easy to move them when you're vacuuming the room, so you can clean under the bed every week. The kids will all want them because you can kick off from the walls and scoot around the room on them when you're supposed to be asleep.

"And the punch-line is: if a kid is scared of a monster during the night, Mum or Dad can just whisk the bed aside and show them — look, no monster."

Of course, Mum or Dad would think that's because the monster was never there. You and I know that it's because as soon as the monster gets into the light — *poof!* It vanishes. And Clyde knows that, too — when he's not trying to be Mr Grown-Up.

So like I said, it makes sense.

Except that, if the monsters were organizing, I didn't think an extra-light bed on wheels was going to stop them. I told Clyde so.

And he said, like he was my favourite uncle or something, "Jack, believe me, when you get to my age you'll realize that monsters under the bed are really nothing to worry about."

"Yeah, Clyde?" I snapped back. "So how come you still keep floodlights on under your bed all night?"

"There's no point talking to you, is there?" he spluttered, going bright red again. "You're just a kid! What do you know?"

"I know *plenty*, Clyde!" I yelled. "I know that monsters are *real*, and they're *dangerous*, and if you could think about anything else except filling your office with presents from your rich daddy, you'd be as worried as I am! Well, I've got news for you, Clyde! All this stuff you've got won't make you any smarter, or any better, and it *certainly* won't make you any more popular!"

He blushed so hot I could have fried an egg on his face.

"You are *so* immature," he said. He turned and looked out the window so I couldn't see how embarrassed he was.

I took the opportunity to lean over his desk, slide his drawer open, and swipe the magazine he'd been reading when I came in.

"Anyway," he said, his voice going just a bit wobbly, "once every kid in the country has a Pumfrey-Soames skatebed, we won't need any registered Monster Investigators, will we? Think about that, Slater. And only the kids I like will get jobs in the new improved Ministry."

I gritted my teeth.

"You trying to threaten me, Clyde?"

"Just telling it like it is, kid."

"You can have this back now, then," I said, and flung my badge on the desk. It skidded across the polished surface and fell on the floor. "Save you the trouble of asking for it later."

I didn't look round as I left the office.

I flicked through the magazine – *Cool Stuff for Kids* – when I got home. It was absolutely what I'd have expected Clyde to read, all about the latest toys and games and gadgets and clothes – everything that a kid might want and money can buy.

He'd circled some of the best stuff. There was a double ring round an item about the new, not-yet-released I-Zak 750 – a combination mobile videophone, games platform, MP3-player . . . you name it, the I-Zak can do it. Press the right button, it'll probably walk the dog and tease your sister for you, too. Just the sort of thing Clyde loved to have, to show off about how rich and important he was.

If he wanted an I-Zak soon, though, he was going to be disappointed. Apparently the test-model they'd made had been stolen from right by the inventor's bed in the middle of the night, while he was fast asleep. They reckoned it was going to take him three months to build another one as good, and another three to get it into the shops. Oddly, Clyde had put a tick and a smiley face next to that bit. Maybe six months was just in time for his birthday. Who knows?

I threw the magazine down. I had more important things to think about than Clyde's I-Want list. The way I saw it, nobody else was going to do anything, so it was up to me. Calling all the other Monster Investigators was out of the question. Even if I hadn't resigned, Clyde was the only one who knew all their names and phone numbers.

So there was only one thing to do.

Chapter Four

If you're going to face down monsters, you've got to be properly dressed. And that means just one thing.

Pyjamas.

Not just any old jim-jams, though. As soon as evening fell, I slipped into my Slater Specials: the Night Operations Utility Pyjamas, their strong fabric hiding all the equipment I needed – each item in its own hand-stitched pocket.

A

B

E

C

D

Penlight torch, spare batteries, Ministry-issue night vision goggles, extra-strong string, Swiss army knife – you name it, I had it. And, of course, Freddy the Teddy.

Yeah, yeah, I know it sounds completely goofy. Jack Slater, big tough Monster Investigator, goes to bed with a teddy in his pocket.

But remember what I said before? Most of the stuff kids make up to stop themselves being afraid of monsters really does work. And how many of you have a special toy in your bed to help keep the monsters away?

It can't just be any old toy, though. The more cuddled and loved it's been, the better. I'd had Freddy since I was a baby, and together we'd seen off a lot of monsters. Teddies, snugglies, even pillows – if it's soft and cuddly and a kid loves it, monsters will hate it.

When I came back from brushing my

teeth, there was a note sticking out from under my bed. Written in the same monstrous handwriting as before, it said:

No mor baj,
no mor monstr
investigater.
wel dun.
plesunt dreems,
litel boy.

Pleasant dreams yourself, I thought, switching off my monster traps and getting ready for bed. I wonder how they found out so quickly?

It came around midnight.

I was lying awake, listening, when there was a scratching sound from under my bed. Suddenly, something scuttled out and darted up onto my pillow.

"Ha! Goodbye, Monster Investigator!" it shrieked, and sank its long pointed fangs into my head.

"Eeeek!" it continued, as my head went *BANG!*

"Erk!" it went on, as someone grabbed it from behind.

"Don't move!" the Someone hissed.

And that Someone, of course, was me. You see, the "head" the little creep had punctured – well, that was just a balloon, part of the dummy I'd put together for just this kind of situation. My real head had been with the rest of me, lying on the floor on the other side of the room, wearing the night vision goggles and waiting for the monster I was sure would come.

You don't get to be the world's greatest
Monster Investigator without making a
few enemies.

Not that I recognized this little squirt,
mind you. But then, no monster who's
actually faced me is going to come back
for a second go, are they?

The little horror froze as instructed –
for all of ten seconds. Then, quick as a
flea, it twisted round and sank its teeth
into my arm.

Except it wasn't my arm.

"Aaaaaaugh!" it yelled, spitting and
yowling.

"Now, that wasn't nice," I said
disapprovingly. "Poor Freddy! I've had him
since I was a baby, you know."

"Help! Help! Get it off my teeth!" the monster howled, as it realized what it had in its mouth. At least, I think that was what it said, although it sounded more like, "Hef! Hef! Ef if off i eef!" Freddy was so well-loved that, to a monster, a mouthful of him must have been like biting on barbed wire.

"Yeah, yeah, in a minute," I answered. It must have been in agony by now, but I didn't care. In fact, I felt a lot worse about letting the little beast puncture my poor teddy, but Freddy's a trooper. He's survived worse.

Still holding the monster by the fur, I reached down beside the bed and flicked a switch.

"Now," I went on, "let me fill you in on a few things. You listening?"

The monster nodded its head, wide-eyed and terrified.

"First," I told it, "I've just put a light on under the bed. There's a light on outside the bedroom door too, and a streetlight right by the window. I can open the curtains and show you if you like."

The little monster shook its head frantically.

"So you're trapped in here with no way out," I told it. "Understand?"

It nodded again, eyes even wider – except for the one in the middle of its forehead, which was blinking rapidly as if it was trying not to cry.

"OK," I said, "you're going to be a good little monster for Uncle Jack, aren't you?"

By this time all three eyes were blinking and filling up. "Ef," it whispered, which I took to be a "yes".

I kept my eyes on it, and one hand on the torch, while I gently pulled Freddy off its fangs and carefully stowed him back in my pocket.

"What's your name?" I asked.

"Seymour," it whimpered.

"Well, Seymour," I suggested, "why don't you and I take a little trip to the monster underworld together?"

Both his mouths fell open, which was a surprise to me as I'd only noticed the one with the fangs. The second was much smaller, with no teeth worth speaking of.

huh.?

huh.?

"Here's what we'll do," I went on. "I'll switch off the light under the bed, and you take me there – but somewhere nice and quiet, with no other monsters around. Deal?"

Seymour's mouths snapped closed again, one after the other. Then the big one opened again.

"Um, um, OK, yeah, yeah," he said, his words racing out like kids at playtime, "yeah, I take you, I take you there but you gotta let me go, OK? You gotta let me go—"

I held up the penlight, and he shut up.

"Seymour, old pal," I told him, "I don't think you're in any position to make demands."

He nodded dumbly, his eyes fixed on the torch.

"I'll do what's right, and I'll play fair," I went on, "but I'm not going to forget that you tried to use my face as a dental brace. Now, let's go."

I fitted a collar and lead to Seymour, pointed the torch at him again, and switched off the light under the bed.

"No funny business," I warned him. "Lead on."

Seymour squirmed under the bed. I followed, the penlight aimed at his back.

It was dark. *Really* dark. Even with the night vision goggles on, I could just about see Seymour, but nothing else.

Which must be why I didn't see how it happened. But after a minute or so we were still crawling forwards, and we hadn't hit the bedroom wall yet. And then I became aware that it was colder, and that I could hear a far-off *drip drip drip* sound.

And that the carpet was gently wriggling beneath my fingertips.

We were in the monster underworld.

chapter Five

I yanked on the lead, and Seymour stopped.

"Where exactly are we?" I whispered.

"Monster underworld, yeah, yeah, in the monster underworld," he jabbered. "You maybe gonna let me go now maybe, please, please?"

I stood up slowly, my hand above my head, feeling for the ceiling. There was plenty of headroom.

"Not yet, Seymour," I told him. "First, you're going to show me what they do with the bad monsters. You know, the monsters who break the monster rules."

The goggles were adjusting to the incredible darkness now. I could see

Seymour thinking about what I'd just asked for. Then he shrugged his shoulders.

"Monster prison? OK," he said, and trotted off. I followed.

Just round the next corner, he jumped on me.

The little rat caught me off guard. The penlight flew from my hand, and within seconds I was on my back with those stiletto-sharp fangs just inches from my face.

"Ha!" he crowed. "Not such a big big-shot now, Mr Monster Investigator, hey? Hey? Not so big now, no. Now I be the hero, yeah, big-shot monster me, yeah, yeah, the monster who finished off Jack Slater, oh yes, all those big monsters who push me around, they gonna treat me with more respect, hey?"

You know, I'd love to tell you about the clever move I made that got me out of

this one. Like maybe I made some funny wise-crack, and then came up with some really smart trick that Seymour hadn't been expecting?

Except I can't, because it didn't happen. What happened was me trying to hold Seymour off, but the creep was stronger than he looked – a *lot* stronger – and those fangs were inching closer and closer every second, slobbering slime onto my face. I was straining and pushing, trying to hold him off, keep him away, and all the time I was thinking, how undignified for the world's greatest Monster Investigator to be finished off by a little squirt like Seymour . . .

. . . and then there was a very menacing click, like someone snapping a battery-cover shut, from somewhere just behind Seymour's head. Seymour froze.

He was getting very good at that.

A cold, hard voice whispered, "Now, I know what you're thinking. You're thinking – 'she's been down here three days. Those *can't* be fresh batteries she's just loaded – can they?' Well, you know what?

In all this excitement, I kind of lost track myself. But considering this is a Night Blaster 35 – the most powerful hand-torch in the world, and could light you up like the Blackpool Tower from half a mile away – what you have to ask yourself now is: 'Do I feel lucky?' Well, do you – punk?"

Seymour made a funny sort of squeaking noise. Then there was a *THUNK!* as he fainted clean away and rolled off my chest, hitting the floor.

"Thanks," I said a little shakily, picking myself off the floor and checking my face for punctures. There weren't any. "Nice speech," I added.

"Thanks yourself," she answered – and now that she wasn't whispering it was easy to tell she was a girl. "I got it off a cop movie."

I looked at her properly for the first time. She was about my age, kitted out in

combat nightie and padded slippers,
wearing night vision goggles and a
backpack shaped like a cuddly pig.
In one hand was a huge torch. Her hair
and skin were so dark it was difficult to
see her even with the goggles on full –
except when she smiled and her teeth
showed up, bright and white.

"Cherry Jackson," she said, sticking out
her free hand. "Official Government
Monster Investigator. You're safe with me."

"Jack Slater," I told
her, taking the
hand and
shaking it.
"Freelance
Monster
Investigator.
You're even
safer with me."

She laughed
again and said,

"There's no such thing as a freelance M.I."

"There is since this afternoon," I told her. "I threw my badge at Clyde and walked." She looked at me to see if I was joking, and decided I wasn't. I could tell she was impressed. "But enough about me," I went on, "let's deal with Seymour here."

I looked down at Seymour and nudged him with my foot. He was still out cold.

"Well, I say we put his lights on – permanently," she said, and reached down to pick up my penlight.

I got to it first. "Not so fast," I told her. "The little rat may have tried to double-cross me, but I still need him." I filled her

in about Bernard, and how I reckoned Seymour could help me find him.

She nodded. "OK, then we need to restrain him," she said, taking off her cuddly backpack pig. "And I think Mr Piggy here has just the thing – don't you, Piggy?" She unzipped him and drew out a thin, threadbare-looking blanket. "It used to be my mum's," she said, "and before that, my grandma's, not to mention all the aunts, uncles, brothers and sisters. This particular blankie has kept three generations of my family safe from monsters over the last seventy years."

Wow. All the cuddles and love and trust it must have soaked up. If that didn't keep Seymour wrapped up and on his best behaviour, I thought, nothing would.

I helped Cherry wrap Seymour up in the blanket, tying it tightly with the string I'd brought with me for just this sort of situation.

"So – have you really been down here for three days?" I asked her, helping her to stuff Seymour into Mr Piggy so only his head showed.

"Yep. Some little weasel of a monster turned up in my room and stole my brand new trainers. I chased the thing under the bed, hoping to catch it, and ended up down here. I've been trying to find my way back ever since."

Now that was weird. What would a monster want with a pair of trainers? Maybe they were linked to the Ghost Burglars after all.

"Well, if we find Bernard he can show us both the way home. But before we do — I've got to know: those batteries you just loaded into your torch . . . *were* they fresh?"

She grinned, lifted the torch and pulled the switch.

In the heart of the bulb, the tiniest of glows flickered just for a moment, and died.

"You can't change the batteries in these babies," she said. "You have to recharge 'em from the mains."

Once Seymour had woken up, we got going quickly. The weaker a monster is, the lighter it gets — don't ask me why —

so he wasn't hard to carry, and just a few minutes later we found ourselves looking down a long thin corridor carved out of rock. Or maybe chewed out of rock, judging from the tooth-marks on the walls.

"Monster prison down there, OK, down there," Seymour moaned. "Now maybe you'll let me go, maybe now, huh?"

"Button it, Seymour," I snarled, "or you'll get a mouthful of teddy."

He buttoned it.

"How many guards do you think there'll be on the place?" Cherry asked me.

"Too many," I answered.

We set off nervously down the corridor. Between us, we had one torch and a guide who'd drop us both in it first chance he got. Our mission: to rescue a monster we wouldn't even recognize if he crawled out

from under our beds waving a sign that said, "It's me, folks!" Following which we had to find out what the other monsters were planning, stop them, and then get home safely.

Personally, I didn't think we stood a chance.

Chapter Six

Of all the tunnels and rooms we saw in
the monster underworld, those in the
monster prison were the most cheerful.
Everywhere else was drab and gloomy, but
someone had gone to the trouble of
decorating this place with
flowery wallpaper.

Admittedly the flowers were all a greeny-
grey colour – but then everything shows
up greeny-grey through the night vision
goggles, and I was prepared to bet that to
the imprisoned monsters they'd be candy-
pink, or something even more jolly. They'd
hate that.

Maybe that was why the first
guard to come round the
corner looked so mean.
We could tell he was
a guard by the big
bunch of keys he
had jangling on
a chain, hanging
from a ring through
his enormous nose.
Quickly, I raised the penlight.

"Hide Seymour!" I shouted to Cherry,
who was several paces ahead. Then I slid
the switch forward.

And nothing happened.

Well, when I say nothing happened, I mean nothing happened with the torch.

Plenty happened with the monster.

It roared, shook its great shaggy head – and charged.

This was one speedy monster, and I had nowhere to hide. It pelted towards me like an express train, filling the narrow corridor with its enormous bulk, bellowing

with gleeful anger. As it came it raised its arms, and sharp, dagger-like claws shot out from its gigantic paws – ready to tear me apart. Cherry ducked and rolled as it hurtled past her, but it was me it wanted – I was the one who'd threatened it – so it flicked her aside like an unwanted bogey and reached out its huge hairy mitts. Its claws swished through the air inches from my face as I leaped frantically backwards. For the second time in half an hour, I thought my time had come.

And for the second time, it was Cherry who saved me.

The way the monster had tossed her aside, she could have been knocked out – she should at least have been knocked breathless – but luckily for both of us, she landed on Seymour. She rolled, and drew her torch as she came up.

"Freeze!" she yelled furiously. The monster stopped, and looked round.

Cherry was kneeling just a few feet away, looking meaner than I've ever seen anybody look – meaner even than our headteacher that time someone widdled all over the floor in the boys' toilets. Her hands were rock-steady, and the bulb of that huge torch was pointed straight at the monster's head. It turned, slowly.

"Hey!" it growled. "You the girl been down here three days, lighting up the tunnels!"

"That's me," Cherry said coolly. "Now, put the claws away and keep your paws where I can see them!"

The monster did neither.

"Three days a long time for batteries," it said, its voice rumbling like a cement mixer. "Maybe your torch ran out of power."

"Maybe it has," Cherry agreed, and her voice took on that cold, hard whisper again. "In all this excitement, I kind of lost track myself. But considering this is a Night Blaster 35 – the most powerful hand-torch in the world, and could light you up like you just stepped under a streetlamp – what you have to ask yourself now is: 'Do I feel lucky?' Well, do you – punk?"

The monster paused for a moment, considering this.

Then it chuckled, and nodded its head.

"Yep!" it said, raising all its claws and stepping forward.

And that was when I hit it from behind.

There's no point hitting a monster with something hard and heavy.

So I hit it with Freddy.

THUD! A quick blow to the back of the knee! It stumbled and half-fell. I leaped up, grabbing a handful of monster-fur.

THWACK! A well-loved teddy came down hard on the back of its head. There was a pause . . .

. . . and then it slowly toppled, banging its head on the wall as it fell, and lay still.

"Sorry about that, Freddy," I said, giving him a kiss.

I looked at Cherry, and we grinned with relief, and high-fived.

"Thanks," I said.

"Thanks, yourself!" she answered. "That's some teddy you've got there."

Then, of course, we had to take the guard's keys.

Problem was, the only way to get them was to take the ring out of the monster's nose.

And the catch was on the inside.

We wasted a couple of minutes arguing about whose job it was to snap the catch open. Cherry reckoned it was my job, because she'd saved my bacon twice. I reckoned it was hers because . . . because . . . because it just *was*, OK?

She wasn't convinced.

So, I took off my watch and spent possibly the worst minute of my entire life up to my elbows in monster snot.

"Guess this is what makes you such a good M.I., Jack," Cherry remarked cheerily.

"What is?"

"You really know how to get up a monster's nose!"

I glared at her.

"Button it, Jackson," I said, "or it's *your* turn for a mouthful of teddy."

Luckily for me, just at that moment the ring popped open.

Unluckily for me, this must have tickled the unconscious monster's nose. It sneezed.

I was blown clean off my feet. Well — not *clean*, exactly. In fact, not clean at all.

"Urggh!" I groaned, picking myself off the floor, dripping wet with something I'd rather not describe. "Anyone got a hanky?"

Sadly, no one did. So I had to make do with Seymour. He was remarkably absorbent, really. Of course, I shook him as dry as I could before wrapping him up again in Cherry's blankie and stuffing him back inside Mr Piggy.

Then we went off to look for Bernard.

We found the main chamber of the prison fairly quickly. It took me nineteen tries to find the right key, though.

The door swung open slowly. I held Freddy the Teddy like a club, ready to hit any monster that came charging out at us.

But none did.

The room was huge – about the size of a football field – and it glowed with a faint luminous light like those glow-in-the-dark stickers you get; not enough to make a monster vanish, just enough to make him very uncomfortable.

It was full of monsters.

Luckily for us, they were all chained up. Well – paper-chained, to be precise. They were tied up with streamers and Happy  Birthday banners, with balloons and with wrapping paper. Some were tied to the floor; some were tied to the ceiling; and all around the walls monsters were paper-chained up high, their feet and tails dangling, looking like the ugliest party decorations you ever saw. They were all muttering and murmuring and complaining to each other, but as they saw us the room went quiet – dead quiet.

I cleared my throat.

"Ahem – which one of you is Bernard?" I asked.

They glared at us suspiciously.

"Who wants to know?" growled a slimy-looking eight-armed creature.

"Yeah – what this Bernard guy done?" added one that looked like a two-headed snake with spider-legs.

"Nothing," I said. "We're here to rescue him."

There was a pause while they took this in.

Then a big hairy yeti-type thing way over on the other side of the room raised his head and bellowed, "I'm Bernard!"

"No you're not!" a little three-headed furry blob called out. "*I* am! *I* am Bernard!"

And suddenly the room was filled with the noise of hundreds of monster criminals all shouting out:

"*I* am Bernard!"

"No, *I* am Bernard!"

"You know," said Cherry, "I think I saw this in a film once."

I turned to the monster nearest me, who was bellowing, "*I* am Bernard" as loud as anyone, and pressed the "light" button on my wristwatch. It shut up very suddenly.

"You know," I said to it above the shouting, "this light isn't big enough to light up a whole monster, but I always wondered what would happened if I held it really close to a monster's toes. Or ears," I added, looking down and noticing that it didn't have any toes.

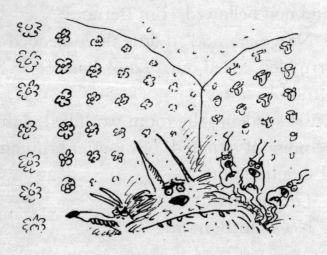

The monster's eyes widened. "Um . . . I might know where Bernard is," it said in a deep, gravelly, but slightly shaky, voice.

"Good boy!" I told it.

"Girl!" it said, offended. "My name's not really Bernard. It's Shirley."

"Nice to meet you, Shirley," I said. "Where's Bernard?"

"Well," she said hesitantly, "I don't know for sure if it's him, but they've been holding someone in that room over there" – she pointed with the one tentacle that wasn't chained to the wall – 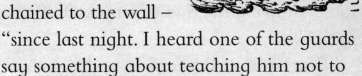 "since last night. I heard one of the guards say something about teaching him not to go blabbing to humans."

"Sounds like it could be him," I said. "Thanks, Shirley. Come on, Cherry."

We made our way carefully across the room, swiping with Freddy at any monster that tried to grab us as we passed.

73

"Bernard?" I whispered, stepping into the room. And then I stopped.

This room was much smaller – about the size of a bedroom. It contained just two things: a lamp, and a monster. The monster was chained to the wall next to the lamp, and he was wearing satin pyjamas and "Timmy the Train" slippers – a monster's idea of torture.

"Bernard?" I said again, louder, and this time he looked up.

"Jack?" he said, and I recognized his voice straight away. I dashed across the room, drawing my Swiss Army knife from its pocket.

"Don't worry, Bernard," I said to him. "We're going to get you out of here. Let's get these pyjamas off you first."

"No – no time!" he said. "The lamp! It's going to go off!"

I looked, and for a moment didn't see what he meant.

Then I realized.
The lamp was plugged in to a timer.
The timer was set for 2:00 am.
I looked at my watch. It was 1:59.
And 55 seconds.
There was no time to get to the plug.
No time to find the switch.
Bernard was about to die.

Chapter Seven

I dropped the knife and dived at the lamp, bringing it crashing to the floor beneath me just as the time-switch clicked.

The lampshade collapsed. I felt the bulb suddenly warm beneath my stomach as it lit up.

"Cherry! Get the plug!" I said, but she was way ahead of me. There was a click from the wall, and then she said,

"OK, Jack – it's off."

I rolled off the lamp and stood up. Bernard was still there, hanging from the wall, grinning at me.

And not looking at all scary.

In fact . . .

"Are you *sure* you're a monster?" Cherry asked suspiciously.

Bernard scowled. He still didn't look scary.

"OK, OK," he growled. "Just because you saved my life doesn't mean you can take the mickey."

We looked at him, unable to believe what we were seeing. He sighed.

"All right," he said. "Here's how it works. Monsters are born from the fears of children. So if a child is scared – *really* scared – of spiders and snakes, then a monster might be born down here with, say, the head of a snake and the legs of a spider."

"That makes sense," Cherry said. "So you were born because some kid somewhere was scared of . . ."

"Yeah, of a cuddly bunny rabbit and a fluffy duck," Bernard snarled. "But he was terrified, OK? Not just scared. Let's get that straight. One kid, once, was really, *really* frightened of me. Now, how about getting me down?" he added, fluffing up the feathers all along his floppy bunny ears.

I popped the balloon and tore off the paper-chains. He ripped off the pyjamas and slippers. There he stood — two metres of cuddly bunny rabbit covered in soft, downy feathers that I'd have been willing to bet were primrose yellow. Cherry and I couldn't help giggling.

"Knock it off, both of you!" Bernard yelled. "Don't you think I get enough of that down here?"

giggle
giggle

"Sorry, Bernard," I apologized. "I guess this is why you decided to become an informer."

"Yeah," he agreed. "Informing gives me something to do. The one kid I'm capable of scaring sleeps with the light on – and soon he'll be too old to believe in monsters. Kids these days grow up too quickly.

I'm telling you, there's nothing more humiliating than—"

"Not now, Bernard," I interrupted. "We've got to get out of here. Can you get us home?"

"Not from here," he said, moving towards the door. "Once we get out, I can get you under any bed anywhere in the world, but the monster prison's escape-proof. How did you get in past all the guards, anyway?"

"Got lucky, I guess," I told him. "We only saw one on the way in."

He stopped and looked at me, like he couldn't believe what he was hearing.

"*One?*" he said. "No way. You should have seen about twenty. Come to think of it, how did you get past the monsters in the tunnels outside the prison?"

I shook my head.

"No monsters," I said. "The tunnels are pretty empty just now."

His face fell. Both floppy bunny ears drooped.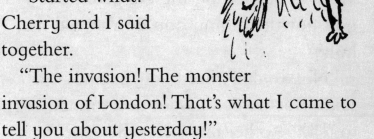

"Awww, *no*!" he exclaimed. "They must have started early!"

"Started what?" Cherry and I said together.

"The invasion! The monster invasion of London! That's what I came to tell you about yesterday!"

This was worse than I'd thought.

"But how *can* they invade?" Cherry asked Bernard. "London's so well lit at night! An army of monsters couldn't ever survive there."

Bernard shook his big bunny head.

"I don't know what the plan is," he said. "But I do know they've got some kind of a secret weapon. And I think I know where to find it — in the New Chamber."

"Yeah, yeah, very nice, big fluffy traitor bunny," Seymour piped up weakly. I'd almost forgotten about him, he'd been so quiet. "What about me, you kids, hey? You gonna keep me tied up in this pig for ever till I die, huh? How about letting me go, yeah? Now you got the bunny you don't need me, huh?"

"No, we don't need you, Seymour," I said. "But we don't want you running off to tell the other monsters where we are. Luckily, Bernard doesn't need these pyjamas any more."

We left Seymour wrapped up and whimpering in Bernard's cell and headed back through the main chamber. As soon as Bernard stepped through the door, one of the prisoners – a huge ugly brute with three heads – yelled, "Hey! It's the Easter Bunny!"

I whipped Freddy out of my pocket.

"Button it, ugly!" I told it. "Or you'll get a mouthful of teddy."

The head that had spoken stared at me, suddenly terrified, while the other two tried to pretend they'd never seen it before – not very successfully, since they were all joined at the neck.

The room was silent as we left. Through the monster underworld we went, until we reached the entrance to the New Chamber.

There was a lot of noise coming from inside.

"Sounds like they haven't left this place unguarded," I said.

"Yes," said Cherry, "so what do we *do*? We need a plan."

I thought for a minute.

"OK," I said, "here's the only thing that makes sense to me. Bernard, you show Cherry the way back home . . . no, *listen*," I added as she started to argue. "Someone's got to warn Clyde, and it's got to be you. He won't listen to me, and Bernard's a monster."

I was right, and she knew it.

"You be careful, Jack Slater," she said. "Bernard'll be back for you in a few minutes. Good luck with the monsters in there."

"Monsters aren't a problem," I grinned, not feeling half as confident as I sounded. "Good luck with Clyde – that's the difficult job!"

I drew Freddy from my pocket again, and pushed open the door.

The first thing I saw, oddly, was a bed –
a Pumfrey-Soames skatebed to be precise
– pushed up against the wall nearby.

The next thing I saw was a monster.

The next forty-three things I saw after
that were also monsters.

And they were all looking straight
at me.

chapter Eight

There was only one thing to do.

As the monster nearest me raised its ugly, cobra-like head to strike, I stepped into the room.

"One . . ." I said loudly.

The monsters looked at each other in puzzlement. On the one hand, I was in the monster underworld, and they had me surrounded . . . but on the other hand, I was in my pyjamas, there was a bed in the room, and they all knew the rules.

"Two . . ." I counted, walking towards the bed as quickly as I could. "Three . . ."

The monsters between me and the bed unwillingly moved out of the way.

"Four . . ." I counted, reaching the bed and hopping into it.

"Five!" I finished triumphantly, tucking myself in. The monsters surrounded the bed, not sure of what to do next. I looked up at them cheerily.

"So . . . what's the plan, monsters? Where's the secret weapon?" I looked round, but couldn't see anything even vaguely weapon-like.

The monsters scowled.

"Can't we eat him?" one of them asked. The others shook their heads.

"He got into bed by five," another said. "It was a fair count."

"But it's *our bed*!" the first one protested.

"Doesssn't matter," a third – the cobra-headed one – hissed. "It'sss alwaysss dark here. No morning. Sssoon he needsss to go to the toilet. We can get him then."

I lay back and looked at the ceiling. They were right – I couldn't stay there for ever. But if I moved, they'd get me. It looked as if my number really was up this time.

And then I heard it – something a trained Monster Investigator has a finely tuned ear for.

A monster had just appeared under my bed.

This was not a serious concern. When you have forty-four monsters gathered around you waiting for you to either starve to death or go for a wee, one more shouldn't be a problem.

And just maybe it might be a help.

"Don't worry, Jack, we'll get you out of this," Bernard's voice said from somewhere below me.

I looked over the edge of the bed. The sheet was twitching.

And then Cherry's face popped out.

"Evening, monsters," she said, pointing her torch at the nearest one. "Just stand back and you won't get hurt."

One of the monsters screamed, "Eeeek! There's a child under our bed!" The one next to it gave it a slap and told it not to be so silly. Keeping the monsters covered, Cherry crawled out and stood up.

Then one of them snarled, "You been down here three days, kid! You got no batteries left!"

Cherry grinned. She was enjoying herself. I wasn't. I didn't think she stood a chance of bluffing her way out of this one.

"That may be so," she said in that quiet, menacing voice. "In all this excitement, I kind of lost track myself. But considering this is a Night Blaster 35 – the most powerful hand-torch in the world, and

could light you up like a pumpkin at
Hallowe'en – what you have to ask
yourself now is: 'Do I feel lucky?' Well,
do you – punks?"

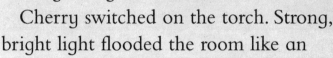

The monsters
lifted their heads
and roared –
an angry,
triumphant roar.

They charged.

Cherry switched on the torch. Strong,
bright light flooded the room like an
instant sunrise.

The monsters
vanished.

Cherry turned
to me with the
biggest grin I'd
ever seen.

"We decided Clyde would be useless,"
she said. "So we went back to my room
and picked up my spare torch."

I grinned back. "Cool," I said. "Nice rescue. Thanks."

"No problem. Actually, it was kind of fun. So . . . what's the secret weapon, Jack?"

I was about to tell her that I didn't have a clue, when a horrible thought suddenly struck me. I felt myself turn pale.

I *did* know what the secret weapon was.

I was sitting on it.

Chapter Nine

"Sorry," Cherry said a moment later, "I must have misheard. I thought you just said the monsters could take over the world using a bed on wheels."

"What?" said Bernard anxiously, crawling out from under the bed and unfolding his big bunny-ears. "You mean it's dangerous?"

What?

"Not to you, Bernard," I said, "but just think about it. Why don't monsters explore the house?"

"Simple," Bernard shrugged. "No one wants to risk being lit up. It's safer under the bed . . ." His voice tailed off as he realized what I meant.

"Bernard," I told him, "get us to London — fast!"

As we emerged into the darkness under a bed somewhere, I became aware of a strange sound. A sort of trundling, whirring noise, a bit like very, very quiet traffic.

"Where exactly are we, Bernard?" I whispered.

"A big furniture shop in Battersea," he answered. "Some of the monsters come here to muck about at night when they're not in a scaring mood. It doesn't usually sound like this, though."

Cherry and I wriggled out from under the bed, and a horrifying sight met our eyes.

From the warehouse at the back of the shop, a vast river of Pumfrey-Soames skatebeds flowed out onto the street. Their wheels made a quiet, constant rumble like the warning before the earthquake.

"Hey! You ain't going to leave me here, are you?" Bernard growled. He was still underneath the bed – an old-fashioned iron double, with no wheels. Although it was dark in the shop, the streetlights outside would be bright enough to vanish him. "I mean – talk about ingratitude! I risk my life warning you, nearly get myself lit up—"

rumble rumble rumble

"Not *now*, Bernard," I told him. "Hang on – we'll hail you a cab."

Quickly, Cherry and I dashed across the sales-floor and leaped onto a skatebed as it trundled past.

"Hey!" came a voice from underneath. "Who's that jumping on *my* bed?"

The monster's head popped out from under the side of the skatebed.

"ROAR!" it roared, and looked up at us – straight into the huge shining reflector of Cherry's torch. It just had time to say, "Oh, *poo!*" before – *FLASH!* – it vanished.

The bed glided to a halt, and then there was a *clang!!!* as the bed behind us crashed into our headboard.

"Hey! Why don't you learn to drive!" yelled a voice, and then there was a whole series of clangs and bangs as, behind it, skatebeds piled into one another.

"Bernard!" we yelled.

"Nice plan!" he said, appearing under our bed. We started to roll forward again, and after a moment the column of beds behind us did the same. "Where to?" he added, as we passed through the doors of the shop and bumped off the kerb onto the road.

"Follow those beds!" I said grimly.

97

At every junction, we met up with more and more Pumfrey-Soames skatebeds, until ours was just one of thousands, wheeling through South London towards the river.

And soon we realized where we were heading.

"Parliament!" whispered Cherry, pointing. There, on the other side of the river, Big Ben stood tall and proud – unaware of the vast army of monsters rolling towards Westminster Bridge.

The vast army of beds wheeled slowly and threateningly up to the entrance to

the House of Commons. And there the
great monster master plan for the invasion
of Britain hit its first problem.

"Humph!" growled a monster under one
of the front beds. "It all shut up! It night-
time. No one here!"

There was a pause, and then a noise like
several monsters hitting whatever they
used for foreheads with whatever they
used for hands.

Then another monster said, "I know!
Let's invade to the Crime Minicab's
house!"

There was a noise like several dozen monsters scratching whatever they used for heads, and then another voice said,

"Who?"

"You know," said the one who'd suggested it. "The Crime Minicab! The top banana! The bloke what tells the governmenty people what to government!"

There was another pause, and then the first voice rumbled, "You so dim, Cynthia! Not Crime Minicab! You mean Prime Miniskirt!"

"Prime Mini-*stir*!" another voice growled.

"Ah-hah!" chorused a number of others. "Yes! Let's go invade to the Prime Minister's house!"

The leading beds wheeled round again.

We were headed for Downing Street.

Chapter Ten

The policeman outside number 10 Downing Street turned as the first line of beds rounded the corner, and his jaw dropped – or at least it would have done if the strap of his helmet hadn't been holding it up. British policemen are well trained, but not for the sight of an army of monsters under beds coming for you and bringing the beds with them. So he did what anyone with any sense would have done in his place.

He rang the doorbell as hard as he could.

Cherry and I saw our chance. "Meet us inside, Bernard!" I hissed, and with a running leap we were both on the road ahead of the beds and racing towards the policeman.

The monsters in the lead were taken by surprise.

"Children!" one of them yelled out. "Where they come from?"

"Out of a mummy's tummy, I think," another one said.

"You *so* thick, Cynthia!" growled the first. "You put children *in* the tummy, not take them out!"

"Never mind that," a third shouted, "they getting away! Chase them!"

And they did. We belted along Downing Street with the skatebeds bearing down on us – fast. They'd have caught us if bumping up the kerb hadn't taken them vital seconds.

"Hey!" I shouted.

The policeman inside number 10 had just opened the door for the one outside, who was quickly stopping being an outside policeman and starting to be another inside policeman. They both halted and looked at each other, and that gave us just enough time to squeeze past them before they shut the door. The first bed slammed into it as it closed.

"Hey, you two!" one of them exclaimed. "Don't you know where you are? You can't just barge in here like that!"

Cherry flashed her "Government Appointed Monster Investigator" badge.

"We're here on Ministry business," she told them.

One of the policemen examined the badge.

"Well, it looks real enough," he admitted. "But everyone knows there's no such thing as monsters."

Just then, there was a loud *BANG!*

The front door shook as the bed slammed
into it again.

And again.

And again.

"Tell *them* that," I said.

The door suddenly and violently
exploded inwards. The skatebeds advanced
upon us.

"Run!" screamed the first policeman.

"Where to?" screeched the second.

"The stairs!" I yelled, and we sprinted.

Down the corridor we pelted, the
skatebeds clattering furiously behind us,
bumping each other as they chased us,
until we saw the stairs ahead of us.

The policemen leaped.

I leaped.

Cherry tripped and fell.

"Dinner!" bellowed the
monster under the first
bed, bearing down
on her.

"Time to
go on
a diet!"
I yelled,
turning
and

hurling myself at the bed. I grabbed at it
as it reached her, catching my ribs on the
frame and slowing it just for a second. A
hot bruising pain burned across my chest.
Cherry scrambled to her feet.

The bed bucked and jolted savagely as the monster tried to shake me off. Then the beds behind slammed into it, taking my breath as they hurled me against the stairs.

"Up you come, son!" one of the two policemen said. They grabbed my arms and hauled me upwards onto the stairs just in time. The bed jerked and lurched, the monster below it trying to reach me – and then it lifted a little too high. I caught a glimpse of a jagged purple claw as the light hit it, and the bed crashed to the floor, suddenly still.

We sat for a moment, half-way up the flight of stairs, as the first few monsters clattered about under their beds in the corridor below.

"What we do now?" one of them muttered.

"Dunno . . . oh, yeah, I remember," said another. "Hey, you!" it called. "We want to speak to the Prime Minister!"

"Er . . . we'll tell him, then," one of the policemen said. "Come on, kids, this way."

We could still hear the monsters below us clattering and muttering as we climbed the stairs and hurried along a wide, portrait-lined corridor to a very grand bedroom door. One of the policemen knocked.

"Umm . . . errr . . . whassat . . ." said a sleepy voice, and then a moment or two later, "Enter!"

We went in. The Prime Minister, his hair sticking out in all directions, was starting to sit sleepily up in bed.

"Um . . . Constable," he said, blinking, "why are you bringing two strange children into my bedroom? And why isn't one of you standing outside the front door?"

"Well – there isn't a front door, Prime Minister. Not any more. Some very fierce beds have broken it down, and now they're at the bottom of the stairs demanding to see you."

The Prime Minister sat up properly and turned the light on. He was wearing purple silk pyjamas with *PM* embroidered on the pocket.

"Very fierce beds? What *are* you talking about? And who are these children?"

"Jack Slater, Monster Investigator," I told him. "This is my colleague, Cherry Jackson." Cherry stepped forward and showed him her badge.

"I see . . ." the Prime Minister said, looking at it, in a voice that meant he didn't see at all. "But, hey, look, kids, surely you know that the Ministry of Monsters isn't a real Ministry at all . . . because, let's face it, there aren't really any monsters under the bed—"

"Oh, ain't there, Mr Clever-Dicky Prime Minister?" growled a voice from somewhere underneath him. The Prime Minister squeaked and leaped out of bed as if a bug had just bitten him.

"What was that?" he yelped,

skittering over to the other side of
the room and hiding behind
a policeman. Cherry
reached for her torch and I
pulled out Freddy the
Teddy, ready for trouble.

"That was me," the voice
said, accurately but unhelpfully.
"Come to tell you what we
want."

The Prime Minister's mouth
dropped open, but no sound came out. I
thought I'd better help.

"OK," I said, "the PM's listening. Tell us
what you want and then beat it!"

The monster chuckled.

"You that Monster Investigator kid!" it
rumbled. "Jack Slater! One day maybe we
have you for dinner!"

"Try it, buster," I warned him, "and
you'll get a mouthful of teddy."

The monster growled softly.

"OK, Prime guy," he went on, "here's what we want. You look outside, you see we got you surrounded. Monsters everywhere. You go downstairs, we eat you. You go out of the house, we eat you. So you got to give up, see? "What we want when you give up, is this:

"First, you gotta stop bein' Prime Minister. We gonna have a Prime Monster instead, see? To tell everyone what to do.

"Second, you gotta turn off all the electradicity. No more lights at night-time. Then we can come out from under the bed and eat the children. Not all the children, 'cos we ain't greedy. Just some of them.

"Umm . . . the one after second, you gotta get rid of all them nasty torches.

"And, ummm . . . That's it. Unless maybe we think of something else, OK? You wanna talk to us, we's at the bottom of the stairs. And outside of the window. You wanna call your friends to help you think, we let them in and not eat them. Yet. You got till the sun comes up to make up your mind."

There was a shuffling sound, and then the monster had gone.

I looked at the Prime Minister. He'd turned completely pale. So had the policemen.

"What do we do, sir?" one of them asked.

"I don't know," he replied shakily. "I really don't know."

What we did was wait.

The policemen went to stand guard outside the bedroom.

Cherry tried to keep her eyes open, but she couldn't. No wonder – after three days in the monster underworld, she must have been exhausted. Soon she was curled up in the corner, snoring gently.

I sat quietly, thinking.

What I was thinking was this:

Something wasn't right. These monsters – even the ones in the lead, the ones making all the decisions – were really thick. Most of them weren't smart enough to count their own fingers – even the ones with *no* fingers. They just weren't clever enough to have planned the invasion.

So, who had?

Chapter Eleven

I must have dozed off.

I was woken by a boot in my aching ribs and a heavy weight landing on me with a thump. Something small and hard bounced off my forehead and skidded across the carpet. I jerked myself awake, half-expecting to find some monster had crawled out from under the bed and caught me napping.

It was worse than that.

It was Clyde.

He'd come rushing in and tripped right over me.

"You idiot, Slater!" Clyde complained. "What's the idea, lying there where any fool could trip over you?"

"Yeah, well any fool just did," I groaned, clutching my ribs. Across the room Cherry sat up blearily, woken by all the noise.

"Well, if we could get on," the PM said, "there's the little business of a monster invasion to cope with. Clyde, as you're the Minister for Monsters, I'd like your opinion on the monsters' demands."

"Oh, yes," Clyde said. He was trying to look grown-up and responsible, but he looked more like a little kid in the headteacher's office trying to explain how come the dog ate his homework *again*. "Let's see: they want power, they want darkness, and they want to eat children.

Umm . . . pretty standard demands in these cases, really."

"*In these cases?*" I burst out. "*What* cases? Clyde, nothing like this has *ever* happened before and you know it!"

Clyde scowled. "I'm the Minister, Slater," he said uncomfortably. "You're just an *ex*-Investigator. So shut up. As I was saying, Prime Minister, this is more or less what they ask for every time. The difference is — this time they have us surrounded."

"Yeah," I muttered, thinking of the skatebeds, "and whose fault is *that*?"

Clyde went red and tried to pretend he hadn't heard.

"Now, I've – I've studied the situation from every angle, Prime Minister," he stammered. "Those beds are light, but they're strong. We could try blowing them up, but we might kill too many innocent people. We could try sending police officers to lift up the bedclothes and let in the light, but the monsters could probably grab them *through* the material and pull them under the bed. We might easily lose our entire police force that way, and still not solve the problem."

"Thank you, Clyde," the Prime Minister cut in impatiently, "but a list of ideas that *won't* work isn't really what I had in mind. What I need from you right now is some advice as to how to defeat the monsters. Well? What *should* we do?"

Clyde shuffled his feet and looked down at the carpet. Once more I was reminded of that kid who hadn't done his homework. Then he spoke again, in a voice so small I could only just hear what he said.

"I don't know."

"Clyde," the Prime Minister said quietly, "this is extremely serious. The monsters under the bed have us surrounded. They have given us until sunrise to agree to their demands. You know more about these creatures than I do. You're my expert. Tell me what you think I should do."

Clyde didn't look up. When he spoke this time, it was no more than a whisper.

"Give up," he said.

There was a stunned silence, broken only by the sound of Clyde sniffing self-pityingly.

"*What?*" the Prime Minister said.

I can't tell you how angry I was.

"I don't *believe* you, Clyde!" I yelled. "Yesterday it was, 'When you get to my age, monsters under the bed are nothing to worry about,' and now it's, 'Oh, we must all lie down and let them eat us!' What's *wrong* with you? What do you think you're . . . you're . . . ?"

My voice tailed off as I noticed something on the floor nearby. Something small and hard that Clyde must have dropped when he tripped over me. I reached out and picked it up.

It was an I-Zak 750.

The very latest must-have item for the kid who had too much already.

The one that wasn't in the shops yet.

Because the prototype had been stolen from the inventor's bedside.

I looked at it, and felt the last piece of the puzzle click into place.

I knew now who the brains behind the monster invasion was.

It was Clyde.

Chapter Twelve

"You selfish, big-headed *idiot*, Clyde!" I roared, leaping to my feet and pushing him in the chest so that he staggered back.

"Look, take it easy, Jack!" said the Prime Minister. "You may not like Clyde's advice, but hey, really, we're in a very difficult situation here. Some hard choices may have to be made, you know, and that's not anybody's fault."

"Yes it is!" I said. "It's Clyde's fault! *All* of this is Clyde's fault! Because he planned this invasion! *He's working with the monsters!*"

Clyde went red.

"You shouldn't even *be* here!" he muttered. "Don't you *dare* start accusing me! You don't know anything about it!"

122

"I know *all* about it!" I yelled at him, waving the I-Zak 750 in his face.
"I know that this is yours! I know how you got one, when they won't be in the shops for another six months! And I know what you gave them in return!"

I *knew* I was right. It all made sense. The stuff in Clyde's office – the I-Zak 750 – the Ghost Burglaries – monsters stealing Cherry's trainers . . . the only explanation was this:

The monsters were stealing for Clyde.

And in return, Clyde had planned the monster invasion for them.

Yes, it definitely made sense.

Try explaining that to a grown-up, though.

"Look, Jack," the PM went on, "we're all upset about this. But, I mean, do you really think a human is going to betray us to the monsters under the bed?"

"Yes, Slater," Clyde agreed, suddenly back in pompous mode. "Do try to keep up. These are monsters. There's no *way* any human being is going to help them, now is there?"

"That ain't what I heard," a gruff voice said from under the bed.

"Bernard!" Cherry exclaimed happily.

Bernard!

"I was getting worried about you! Where've you been?"

"Talking to people," Bernard

explained. "Monster people, that is. Tryin' to get a handle on what's happening. And I'm hearing some very interesting gossip."

"Hold on a moment," the Prime Minister said. "Who's this?"

"Bernard's on our side," I answered, still glaring at Clyde. "He was the one who warned us about the invasion in the first place. If he says he's got information, it'll be worth hearing."

"Well, if he's our friend," the Prime Minister said, "I really think he ought to come out where we can see him."

"If you want to see Bernard," I told him, "we'll have to put the lights out. And you'll need night vision goggles."

"I've got a spare pair," Cherry offered, fishing them out of her backpack, Mr Piggy.

"Fine," the PM said, putting them on, "thank you."

Clyde very reluctantly put his on too, and the PM put the lights out.

"OK, um, Bernard," he said. "All the
lights are off. If you want to talk to us, I'm
afraid you'll have to come out."

There was a pause. I felt sorry for
Bernard – after all, when a monster comes
out from under the bed, no one expects it
to look like a feathery bunny. Out he
came, glaring and daring us to laugh.

But before he could speak, a piercing
scream split the air.

A scream of pure terror.

Chapter Thirteen

"No!" shrieked Clyde. "NO! NOT . . . *MR BUN! MR BUN!!!! AAAAAAAGH!!!!!!*"

Everyone turned to look.

"Hey!" Bernard grinned hopefully. "You're not, um . . . *scared*, are you? Of *me*?" He took a step towards Clyde, and then another.

"*NO! KEEP IT AWAY! KEEP IT AWAY!*" Clyde screeched.

Bernard's grin widened. He bared his teeth.

"Not now, Bernard!" I said, but Bernard was having too much fun.

"Grrrr!" he growled, and when that produced a series of satisfying squeaks from Clyde, he tried, "*RAARRRRRR!*"

"No!" Clyde squealed. "NO!" He turned to me, fear burning in his eyes.

"Keep it away!" he howled in terror. "I'll confess! I'll tell you everything! JUST KEEP IT AWAY!"

"Hold it, Bernard," I said, and turned to Clyde. "Did you just say you'd confess?"

"Everything!" Clyde moaned. "Just keep it away!"

"I tell you what," I told him. "Bernard'll go back under the bed just as soon as you've finished telling us the truth. All of it!"

Clyde looked at me. Then he looked at Bernard.

Bernard grinned.

"Boo!" he said.

Clyde jumped backwards, squealing like a piglet.

"It wasn't supposed to go this far!" he howled. "I gave them the idea – but I didn't think they could do it!"

"What idea?" I asked. I was sure I already knew, but I wanted the PM to hear it.

"For the invasion! I found the plans for the skatebed in my dad's office and I realized how the monsters could use it!"

So Clyde hadn't designed the skatebed himself, I noted.

"And what did you get out of it, Clyde?"

It looked for a moment like he was going to zip his lips, but then Bernard growled softly and the zipper broke wide open.

"All the stuff! All the cool stuff my dad wouldn't buy me! New stuff that no one else at school had! The monsters could go anywhere that had a bed, and get me the things my dad wouldn't! Computer games, designer clothes, DVDs, trainers . . ."

"Not to mention things you can't even buy in the shops yet," I said, holding up the I-Zak. Clyde nodded dumbly. "So this whole invasion – the entire country put at risk - is all about you showing off. The monsters stole whatever you wanted, and you gave them what *they* wanted. That's a fair swap, is it, Clyde? It doesn't matter how many kids are put at risk, as long as they all think you're just *so* great?"

"But I didn't think it would matter!" he sniffled. "I told them how to invade – but I thought they were too stupid to get it right!"

And then he collapsed, and begged me to send Bernard – or "Mr Bun" as he kept calling him – away.

Bernard didn't want to go. Clyde, it turned out, was the kid whose fears – of a toy bunny rabbit and a fluffy duck – had brought Bernard into existence, and it had been years since he'd been able to scare him like that.

"Look, Bernard," I told him, "we've got an invasion to sort out. I can't think with Clyde whimpering like that. Please — just get back under the bed."

Bernard rolled his eyes. "You don't get it, Jack. It's been five years since I last heard that sound. Monsters *need* it. I can't stop now. When am I next going to get the chance? He keeps his room floodlit at night, you know! And who else is ever going to be scared of me?"

"Um, Bernard," the Prime Minister said, "I'm afraid Jack's right. Sorry to spoil your fun, but I'm going to have to put the light on in a moment."

Bernard sighed. "Well, it was fun," he said. "See you around, Jack. So long, Cherry. Nice to meet you, Prime Minister. ROARRRR!" This last was to Clyde, who screamed quite satisfactorily and tried to climb through the wallpaper.

"Take care of yourself, Bernard," I said. "I'll see you if we ever get out of this."

He waved, slipped under the bed and was gone.

Clyde was trembling in the corner, looking utterly wretched.

"I thought they were too stupid!" he whined again.

The Prime Minister looked at him scornfully, and then beckoned Cherry and me aside.

"Um, listen, you two," he said, "we're still surrounded by monsters, and we've got no more than a few minutes till sunrise. You're the only monster experts I have left. Any ideas how to stop them?"

"Hmmm . . ." I said. A thought had just
struck me. "You know, I just might."

I went to the window and heaved it
open. Outside, the street below was
covered with skatebeds, bumping and
rattling impatiently against each other.

"Hey! You monsters!" I called.

"Who? Us?" came a voice from under
one of the beds.

"Well, yes," I answered. "All of you.
We're just wondering up here – what do
you want to get out of this invasion?"

"Oh, that easy!" said another voice.

134

"We want to eat children!"

"Mmmm, yum yum!" came a chorus of monster voices. "Eat children! Yeah!"

"But why?" I asked.

"Duh!" the first voice said. " 'Cos they taste nice, that why!"

"Right," I said, "so you've tasted children then, have you?"

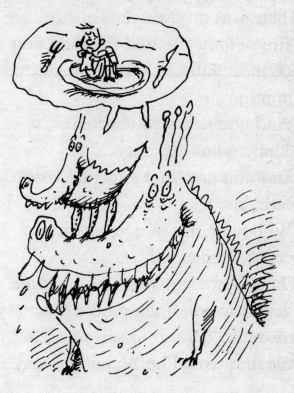

There was a pause, and a lot of muttering. Then the first voice said, "Well . . . no . . ."

"But you know someone who has?" I asked.

"Um . . . no . . ."

"How do you know what children taste like, then?"

There was an awkward silence.

"Er . . . someone told me they taste like chicken," a different voice volunteered hesitantly.

"And you've tasted chicken?"

"Um . . . not exactly . . ."

How can you "not exactly" taste something?

"So how many of you *have* tasted chicken?" I enquired.

The monsters muttered some more. "Um . . . less than one," admitted a voice cautiously.

"So that would be: none?" I asked.

"None of you have ever tasted children; and you think they taste like chicken, but none of you have ever tasted that either?"

"Er . . . yup."

"Why do you want to eat them, then?"

Silence.

One of them said hesitantly,

"Uh . . . dunno, really."

"They just scream so nicely when they're scared," said another.

"Yeah!" agreed the first. "Nothin' in the world sound as good as itty-bitty childern going, 'Eeeeeeeek! There a monster under my bed!'"

"Yeah!" joined in the others enthusiastically. "Best sound in world – ickle kiddies screaming 'cos they afraid of us!"

"And how, exactly," I asked, "will they be able to scream when you've eaten them?"

There was an absolutely horrified silence. It lasted maybe twenty or thirty seconds, as the idea began to percolate through the monsters' tiny little brains.

Then the beds began to rattle and jostle each other angrily.

"Whose stupid idea was this?" shouted a voice.

"I not playing no more," yelled another. "I not eating the kids if they not screaming afterwards!"

"Yeah!" shouted a third. "We not eating childers! Jus' try an' make us, that all!"

The beds rattled angrily once more,

a furious, monstrous sound. The noise swelled like a tidal wave until, for just a moment, it seemed to fill the sky. Then, like the end of a rainstorm, the rattling slowly died down to nothing at all and every bed at last stood absolutely still.

The monsters had gone.

And then the sun came up.

Chapter Fourteen

As you might expect, the Prime Minister immediately offered to set me up as the new Minister for Monsters, in a brand new Ministry, with as much money as I needed to fully train and equip as many Monster Investigators as I wanted.

I turned him down.

brand new MONSTER INVESTIGATORS

Yeah, it could've been fun – but it would never have happened.

You see, the Prime Minister's a grown-up. By lunchtime, he'd have forgotten all about the monster invasion.
He'd have been worrying about how to get all the skatebeds out of Downing Street, but he wouldn't have remembered how they got there.

Because grown-ups don't believe in monsters under the bed. Not in the warm light of day.

Unfortunately, that also meant that he forgot Clyde's part in the whole thing. So Clyde's still the Minister for Monsters, in the treehouse office, with his daddy paying for everything.

That's why Cherry handed in her badge, too. Besides, Clyde still owed her a new pair of trainers.

I suggested something to the PM which he did remember, though.

I suggested he tell his friend, Clyde's dad, that Clyde's too old to have a light on in his room at night. And Clyde's dad agreed.

Which means that Bernard's evenings have been much more fun lately.

Mine haven't. You see, once they'd got all the skatebeds back in the shops, cleaned them up, and put them on sale, they turned out to be a pretty popular piece of furniture with both children and parents.

And with monsters.

So business is busier than ever.

Which is why, a couple of nights later, I was just in the middle of a lovely dream when my

bedroom door opened and the light from the landing woke me up.

I groaned and opened my eyes. Two timid-looking pyjama-clad figures stood there, shuffling sheepishly.

"Um . . . please can we sleep in your room tonight?" one of them said.

I groaned again, and sat up. "What's wrong?" I asked, even though I knew what the answer would be.

"There's a girl under our bed!"

Sighing, I swung my feet out of bed and into my slippers.

"All right," I said. "You two snuggle up in here and go back to sleep. I'll deal with the—"

My mouth paused as my brain hit "replay".

"Mum . . . did you just say there was a *girl* under your bed?"

And then Cherry burst in.

"Eeek!" squeaked my parents, disappearing under the covers. I worry about them sometimes.

"Hey, Jack," Cherry said cheerfully. "Hi, Mr and Mrs Slater. Sorry if I scared you! Let's move, partner, we've got work to do!"

"What?" I complained. "Don't we get a few days off after saving the world?"

Cherry grinned. "Jack," she said, "if we ever save the world, we can take the whole week off. This week we only saved the UK – we don't get any kind of a break for that. Let's get going! Bernard's going to drop us off on his way to Clyde's."

"Drop us off where?" I asked, but she was already heading towards my parents' bedroom.

"Come on!" she yelled over her shoulder. "Last one there's only the world's *second* greatest Monster Investigator! Do you feel lucky?"

"Button it!" I yelled back, putting on a burst of speed. "Or you'll get a mouthful of teddy!"

And, neck and neck, we dived for the space under the big double bed.

ABOUT THE AUTHOR

When John Dougherty was little he wanted to be a superhero, but somehow he became a primary school teacher instead – which isn't quite the same thing. Then he became an author and now he has lots of fun visiting schools to talk about his work. He's also a performing singer-songwriter and occasional poet. John's first book for children, *Zeus on the Loose*, was shortlisted for the Branford Boase Award in 2005. He lives in Stroud, Gloucestershire with his wife and two children.

ZEUS ON THE LOOSE!

John Dougherty

*"I am the great and mighty Zeus, mortal . . .
give me one good reason why I shouldn't
smite you here and now!"*

Alex's class are learning about the Ancient
Greeks. That's why Alex makes a temple
(out of loo rolls and a cornflakes box)
for the Greek god Zeus.

He doesn't expect the god himself to turn up,
borrow his mum's nightie and demand a
sacrifice at half-past five in the morning.
Even worse, Zeus reckons it's time for another
Trojan War – in the school playground!

ISBN 0 552 55081 7/ 978 0 552 55081 9

NITERACY HOUR

John Dougherty

WHAT A LOUSE!

Gregory is a good listener. Jim is
a head-louse, newly-hatched from
a nit on Gregory's head.

As school story time turns into
Niteracy Hour, Jim has breakfast –
and becomes a good listener too!

That's how he hears that big, bullying
Duncan is going to push Gregory's head
down the toilet! Can Jim help Gregory
do something about Duncan –
the real louse in the class?

ISBN 0 552 55082 5/ 978 0 552 55082 6

THE PROMPTER

Chris D'Lacey

"Look out, it's the crocodile!"

Robin is VERY excited when his class
begins rehearsing for the school play,
Peter Pan. But when his acting becomes
a little too energetic, the only role
Miss Everdue can find for him is that
of the play's prompter.

Then disaster strikes the day before
the performance . . .

ISBN 0 552 54934 7 / 978 0 552 54934 9

JOE V. THE FAIRIES

Emily Smith

"There's no such thing as fairies!"

Joe is sure he's right, but his sisters are
obsessed by them. They've turned the
climbing frame into a fairy bower, there
are fairy cakes for tea and no one wants
to do his assault course any more. Then a
new neighbour arrives, who loves climbing
trees and messing about in the pond –
and has some other very useful talents too.

A fantastic story for all fed-up brothers –
and their sisters too – from a two-time winner
of the Smarties Children's Book Prize

ISBN 0 552 55174 0/ 978 0 552 55174 8